RAYMOND

Yann & Gwendal Le Bec

WALKER BOOKS
AND SUBSIDIARIES
LONDON • BOSTON • SYDNEY • AUCKLAND

Raymond was a happy dog.

He was a good dog, too.

He said please, **"WOOF!"**

And thank you, **"WOOF! WOOF!"**

And he never complained,

even when getting his fur trimmed

by the doggy dresser.

Raymond loved his family.

And they loved him, too – very, very much.

They always saved him a snug little spot

by the sofa, scratched behind his ears in just

the right place and, every year, threw him

a surprise birthday party.

It was a pretty nice life for a dog

like Raymond.

But, one day, Raymond had a thought
(a rather **BIG** thought for a dog).
Looking up at his family seated around the
table, and looking down at his bowl of food,
he wondered...

Couldn't I just SIT at the table?
Isn't that what families do together?

With each passing day, Raymond began
to act more and more like a human.
And, soon, so did every other dog in town.

There were cappuccino-and-cupcake Saturdays
at the café and cinema trips with big action
movies and sweet-and-salt popcorn.

The world looked different on two feet,
bigger on two feet.

Raymond felt like he could do anything.

And that was when he spotted
DOGUE magazine...

Raymond felt as if DOGUE had been written just for him:

NEW WAYS TO SURPRISE THE POSTMAN!

HOW TO AMBUSH CATS!

THE BEST DOG FOOD IN TOWN!

ALL THE LATEST DOGGIE FASHION NEWS –

"COLLARS OUT, SUNGLASSES IN."

So when Monday came, and Raymond watched his family

head out for the day, he had another (rather big) thought...

"You're looking for a job, eh?" said the editor-in-chief of **DOGUE** magazine.

"Yes, please," Raymond said, nodding.

"OK. So, tell me, what's your opinion on cats?" he asked.

"Well ... they are *unbelievably* silly," said Raymond.

And the job was his.

Raymond became a full-time **DOGUE** rover-ing reporter and each day brought a new adventure.

He interviewed pooch painters ...

top dog sniffers ...

acrobatic poodles ...

and tail-wagging tycoons.

Raymond was a very good reporter.

He pushed himself to meet deadlines,

working, always working,

to sniff out the next big headlines.

Even at night,
all his family could
hear was Raymond
tap-tap-tapping on
his computer.

He worked himself
to the bone.

Before long, Raymond became the face
of the biggest dog's TV channel around
– **Dog News.**

His family tuned in every night;
it was the only time they got to see
their Raymond.

Soon, *everyone* wanted a piece of Raymond.

His fur wasn't just trimmed – it was washed,
combed and styled, every single day.
It was all becoming a bit too much.

WHAT A DOG'S LIFE.

For his birthday, Raymond's family
finally persuaded him to take a break.

But the whole way there,
Raymond couldn't help panicking
about the work piling up –
the phone calls ... the emails ...
the meetings ... his FUR!

Until ... a ball went *bounce bounce bounce* right by him.

And Raymond felt a familiar feeling.

A feeling he had forgotten all about...

HE JUST HAD TO CHASE THAT BALL!

He had forgotten how **MARVELLOUS** it was

to have his belly scratched!

And what fantastic fun it was

to get his paws dirty!

A DOG'S LIFE WAS ABSOLUTELY BRILLIANT!

And, back home, as Raymond cosied

up in his snug little spot,

he decided that work could wait.

There were much more important things to do...

Like getting your ears scratched,

in just the right place.